RUBY LU, EMPRESS of EVERYTHING

RUBY LU,
EMPRESS of RESS
EVERYTHING

Lenore
Look

Aladdin Paperbacks
New York London Toronto Sydney

Illustrated by
**Anne
Wilsdorf**

To Madison, my first and best reader
—L. L.

ACKNOWLEDGMENTS

Writing a second book to follow a first book is harder than it looks.

First you have to remember what happened in the first book.

Then you have to think of new, and preferably more harrowing, adventures.

Then you have to convince yourself that you want to write
a second book instead of living these adventures.

Because once you've decided to write a second book,
it requires what the first book required: sitting at your lonely
desk for long, lonely hours each day, checking your e-mail
every second. So it helps to have people in your life, like:

REBECCA SHERMAN, my agent's astute assistant,
who gave my first draft a scorching first read, which kept
me from writing a sequel to a book that doesn't yet exist.

SUSAN COHEN, my wonderful agent, who took
Rebecca's side and also took care of everything else.

ANNE SCHWARTZ, my marvelous editor, who loved Ruby
from the start and somehow convinced me that
sitting still can be the biggest adventure of my life.

ANN KELLEY, her very smart assistant, who took over
the editing of Ruby and should be given an award
for her patience, humor, and perseverance.

ANNE WILSDORF, whom I've never met, but who is able
to see exactly what I see, halfway around the world from me.

DIETRICH TSCHANZ, who found the only copy of a pictoral
Chinese Sign Language dictionary in New Jersey
and risked all sorts of library fines by sending it to me.

CHRIS BURANS, 9-1-1 operator #151 in Randolph, New Jersey, who helps
people in need, and repeated the 9-1-1 response to me until I got it right.

Thank you all.

—L. L.

RUBY LU, EMPRESS of EVERYTHING

1

The Best Thing About Immigration

The best thing about having a cousin come from another country to live with you is everything.

Ruby liked the parties. When Flying Duck and her parents emigrated from China to Ruby's house, there was one celebration after another. Every day felt like a birthday.

Ruby liked the noise and excitement. Before she got up in the morning, she could hear grown-ups talking in the kitchen. The telephone rang all the time. The doorbell worked overtime. Everyone wanted to meet the newcomers.

Ruby liked being a tour guide. Flying Duck and her parents had come from a small rural village. Everything in their new American city was strange and fascinating, especially the places on Ruby's tours. They loved to pose with many ordinary things that they thought were extraordinary. Like ferries. And seagulls. GungGung's car. A parking meter. A meter maid. A meter maid scribbling in her notebook. The convict-orange parking ticket on GungGung's wind-shield! Ruby snapped a hundred pictures.

Ruby liked her uncle. He was an expert bike rider, just like Ruby. Once he carried a giant refrigerator on his bicycle. And he had the photo to prove it.

Ruby liked her aunt. She was a mah-jongg master before she became an immigrant. Ruby loved mah-jongg. It was like playing cards, only noisier. And it was very addictive.

"The best way to get to know someone is to live with them and play mah-jongg with them," she told Ruby in Cantonese. Every evening she'd put on a little Chinese music. And serve up a bowl of pumpkin seeds. Then they'd play mah-jongg.

Ruby liked the buddy system. Ruby was Flying Duck's Smile Buddy at school. Smile Buddies were responsible for helping a new student feel welcome. Smile Buddies were friendly and loyal and helpful. They were courteous, kind, and cheerful. They knew the times of lunch and recess and the locations of the bathrooms. They introduced you around. They made everything less scary. Ruby had waited her whole life to be a Smile Buddy.

SMILE BUDDY, said the big, bright yellow grin pin on Ruby's sweater. Ruby wore it every day. She was now as important as a crossing guard. And she adjusted it often, just to make sure it was still there.

Show-and-tell improved quite a bit. For nine days straight, Ruby showed

UtterPrincess, a hyperaction heroine from China that was a gift from Flying Duck. Ruby carried UtterPrincess with her wherever she went, and in her original box to keep her pristine forever.

"UtterPrincess!" Ruby would say, holding up her box so that everyone could see the doll through the plastic window. Ruby turned it this way and that, as if she were holding up a gem and showing off every facet.

"She swims and speed-reads and speaks five languages," Ruby liked to say. But most important of all, UtterPrincess looked like Ruby and Ruby looked like UtterPrincess.

Soccer improved quite a bit too. It was kiddie soccer, so there was no uniform. You could wear whatever you wanted. Usually everyone tried to look like a soccer player in shorts and a T-shirt. But not Flying Duck. She put on her

PINK FLOWERS

PINK SHIRT

PINK RING

PINK BELT

PINK SHORTS

PINK SOCKS

PINK SNEAKERS

pink socks, pink sneakers, pink shorts, pink shirt, pink belt, pink pinky ring, and a pink headband with very large pink flowers that jiggled when she ran. *Boop, boop, boop.* It was Flying Duck's favorite outfit, and she always felt better when she wore it.

Why didn't Ruby think of that? Inspired, Ruby pulled on her green frog-leg tights, green glow-in-the-dark-see-you-a-hundred-miles-away sweater with asparagus-stalk arms and matching asparagus tips on the head that also jiggled when she ran, but not too much. *Woomp, woomp, woomp.* Wow.

ASPARAGUS TIPS

GREEN GLOW-IN-THE-DARK-SEE-YOU-A-HUNDRED-MILES-AWAY SWEATER...

...WITH ASPARAGUS-STALK ARMS

GREEN FROG-LEG TIGHTS

Ruby once hated soccer. But now she loved it, loved it, loved it.

But the absolute best thing about immigration was Flying Duck herself.

Flying Duck was a source of endless fascination for Ruby and her friends on 20th Avenue South. In many ways she was more of a curiosity than even the 110-year-old mummified man at the World Famous Ye Olde Curiosity Shoppe, the best souvenir store in the whole world right there on the waterfront, a mere fifteen-minute drive from Ruby's house. The mummy, next to the cabinet full of shrunken heads, had a bullet hole in his stomach still shiny with blood, but Flying Duck was an entire foreign country unto herself.

She ate one-thousand-year-old eggs for breakfast.

And one-hundred-year-old eggs for lunch.

She could read backward from right to left.

And hold her breath for forty-two seconds.

And play mah-jongg past bedtime without falling asleep.

But that was not all.

She could ward off evil spirits up to one hundred feet with her special jade pendant.

Even better than that, Flying Duck could do something nobody else on 20th Avenue South could do.

She could lip-read.

Lip-reading is a very useful skill. It comes in handy when you want to watch TV, but the TV is supposed to be turned off. And it comes in handy if you are outside looking in and your parents are inside talking about you.

Flying Duck could speak and lip-read Cantonese. And because she had gone to English school in China, she also knew a little English.

Flying Duck was lip-reading even before she went to the Taishan School for the Deaf, where she had learned another amazing thing: Chinese Sign Language.

Flying Duck had been deaf for nearly half her life. When she was four years old, she fell off the roof of her house where she had gone to "inspect" the tasty peanuts that her mother was drying in the sun.

"I burst my skull," Flying Duck said in Cantonese. Then she signed it, tapping her head and making a burst of fireworks with outspread fingers behind her ears. Ruby's neighborhood friends, Tiger, Christina, and Emma, did not understand Flying Duck. But Wally did. Wally was from Hong Kong, and he was fluent in Cantonese.

"She burst her eardrums," Wally translated.

But the best part of the story . . . and Ruby knew exactly how to tell it . . . was . . .

"The whole village thought she was dead."

Everyone gasped. It was the most exciting thing that had ever happened to anybody on 20th Avenue South.

Ruby and her friends were quick to learn their first Chinese Sign Language: wiggle the thumb at the knuckle, it means "thank you." It was easy now for even Oscar and Sam, the babies on the block, to remember their manners. They wiggled their thumbs at everything.

Flying Duck was very pleased.

And Ruby was very proud. Flying Duck was just perfect. Having a cousin from China who was deaf was as good as having a cousin who had a third eye in the middle of her forehead.

2

Afternoon Crafts

Ruby's mother was very talented. She knew an ancient Chinese saying for nearly everything.

"A wonder lasts but nine days," she said, which is the same as saying that even the most interesting things get old—quickly.

Ruby's Snow Queen skates, which made her as slippery as jellyfish on a spoon, had lasted four days.

Samurai Sumo Sidekick, which came with extra batteries, had lasted three.

And Oscar, when he was born, as sweet as a red-bean dumpling, had lasted two.

So it was a miracle that Flying Duck and the marvels of immigration lasted as long as they did.

Then . . . nothing was right.

First, there was the computer. Flying Duck always left it on the Chinese Internet. She loved playing mah-jongg online, and e-mailing her friends in Chinese. Ruby did not.

Second, there was the Cantonese. With the exception of Ruby and Ruby's father, who was a Chinese School FOB (Flunked Out Badly), nobody spoke English at home anymore. Home became a foreign country!

Third, there was the toilet seat. Flying Duck would always leave it up. Chinese toilets require standing on the rim and squatting, which Ruby liked. But . . . Ruby's favorite shoes were ruby slippers that twinkled like a million diamonds. And it was easy to forget to take them off before

balancing on the
toilet rim until . . .
Aiyaaaaah! Splash!

Fourth, there were
the chopsticks. Flying
Duck used them for
everything. She ate her
spaghetti with them. She could pick up a
meatball without spearing it. She could
even pick up . . . a pea. And then one day the
forks disappeared altogether.

"Good for Ruby to practice her chopstick
skills," Ruby's mother announced.

Fifth, there was Ruby's baby brother,
Oscar. He loved sign language. He was
always wiggling his cute little thumbs at
Flying Duck. His signing vocabulary
soon included "more," "eat," "sleep," "dog,"
and "help." He could sign more than he could
speak, and it was more than Ruby could keep

up with. So Flying Duck knew what Oscar needed before Ruby knew. It was not fair.

Before Flying Duck arrived, Ruby's father had told her that immigrants do many things differently. They eat different foods, dress differently, speak a different language, practice different habits. Different didn't mean wrong. It just meant not the same.

Ruby liked different.

She even liked weird.

But Ruby didn't like having her life turned upside down.

"Send her back," Ruby cried one night. She ran into her mother's arms and burst into tears. "I hate immigration!" Ruby sobbed.

Ruby's mother wrapped Ruby in her arms and gave her a kiss and brushed away her tears.

"I know," Ruby's mother said. "Immigration is very scary. And you've been very brave."

Ruby's mother was right. Ruby had been very brave. Every day there had been a new challenge. And every day Ruby had done her best to keep up with the program.

"The worst is probably over," Ruby's mother said. "Everything will start to get easier. You'll see."

Ruby's mother was right. Immigration could hardly get more miserable.

But it did.

Afternoons after school were not the same. Ruby's mother was not there for tea anymore. She was out helping Flying Duck's parents find jobs. Without Ruby's mother at home, PohPoh always had something for them to do.

Crafts.

Flying Duck made necklaces and earrings out of peanut shells. She folded origami. She cut kirigami. She made moon boots from coconut shells. She glued rice into mosaics. There wasn't anything she couldn't make with a few toothpicks or chopsticks or Popsicle sticks.

But Ruby was never good at crafts. And crafts were never good to Ruby. Opening a craft kit was like opening an umbrella on a blustery day. Ruby would always end up flipped inside out.

And Oscar was never much help.

"Bee," Oscar slobbered. He couldn't yet say Ruby, so he called her Bee. He loved his sister. He loved everything she made. And he drooled heavily over everything he loved.

"Not intended for children under three," Ruby warned him.

They were making refrigerator magnets. Ruby read the instructions.

"Swallowing hazard." That meant Oscar could look, but not touch.

"Use special markers to make design.

"Insert design into plastic sleeve right side up.

"Press front onto back.

"Use hot glue gun to attach magnet.

"Enjoy!"

Ruby did not enjoy. She couldn't get her artwork between the plastic. Press back onto front? Forget it. She could hardly tell up from down.

"Wuv," Oscar said, pressing his drooling wet face to the artwork that Ruby had just finished.

"Oh no!" Ruby cried. She could read Oscar's face. It said, "ʎppnꓭ ǝlᴉɯS."

The words "Smile Buddy" had come off on his cheek. Ruby was making a Smile Buddy magnet for their refrigerator.

"Wuv you, Bee," Oscar cooed. He was so happy. He loved afternoon crafts.

"I love you too," Ruby said, letting Oscar smother her with a wet kiss. She couldn't resist.

But her artwork was ruined. Ruby knew Oscar didn't mean it. But the best part of her craft project now looked like washed lettuce, limp and a little dark in some places.

Ruby never wanted to open another craft kit again.

But Oscar did. He was like a little lobster when it came to crafts. He had just discovered that he could use his pointer fingers and thumbs like pincers. He could pick up just about anything and put it anywhere. He especially liked the teeny tiny hockey pucks that clicked together. He pulled them apart. They clicked together.

"Bee, see!" he said, pinching one of the tiny pucks. But Bee did not see.

It was small and round. And it fit perfectly . . . up his nose!

"Ummp," he said.

"See, Eee!" he said, pinching another teeny puck. With a plugged nostril, he could no longer say his *B*. But Bee ignored him.

Oscar smiled. He drooled. He pushed the second dark puck into his other nostril!

Pak! The pucks clicked together inside Oscar's nose.

"Owwwwow!" he said, surprised. He drooled. He breathed through his mouth.

"Help," he signed to Flying Duck. "Help!"

Flying Duck stopped. She looked at Oscar.

"Help!" he signed again. "Help!"

Ruby finally looked at Oscar. She looked him up and down. She turned him around.

Then she looked up his nose. It was dark and mysterious. His nose was as hard as rocks. No one could quite tell what was up there. Whatever it was, it wouldn't budge.

"Call 9-1-1!" PohPoh cried.

Ruby ran for the phone. She never imagined that crafts could be so exciting. She had always wanted to call 9-1-1.

"9-1-1," said the operator. "Where's your emergency?"

"In the dining room," said Ruby. Her heart pounded in her ears. She could hardly hear herself. She was actually talking to the 9-1-1 operator! It was just like on TV!

"Are you at twenty-eight zero seven?" asked the operator.

"Wow," said Ruby.

"Hello?" said the operator. "State your exact location."

"Next to the refrigerator," said Ruby.

"Do you need medical attention?"

"No," said Ruby.

"Does someone there need help?"

Ruby nodded.

"Hello?" said the operator.

"Oscar stuck something up his nose," Ruby blurted. "And he can't breathe!"

Oscar was screaming like a banshee.

Suddenly 9-1-1 wasn't so exciting anymore. Ruby dropped the phone and ran to him.

Poor Oscar. He was very uncomfortable. He couldn't breathe through his nose. And when he cried, he couldn't breathe at all! Help was on the way, but just then he became unusually quiet and unusually purple. Then he was a little limp and a little blue.

"*Aiyaaaaaaaah!*" PohPoh screamed.

Ruby froze. She did not know what to do.

Flying Duck froze too. Then she did something that Ruby had never seen before. It was strange. And it was completely gross. She quickly sealed her mouth over one of Oscar's nostrils and sucked. *Sluuuurp!*

It was a little tricky. Oscar had baby nostrils.

But Flying Duck was a regular vacuum. She had seen mothers in China do this whenever their babies couldn't breathe.

Then . . . *schlooot!* One heavy little pellet slid into Flying Duck's mouth, and she spat it on the table. *Dok!*

Ruby gasped.

Flying Duck moved to the next nostril. *Schlooot!* She spat out the second pellet. And *pak!* They clicked together on the table.

"Our magnets!" Ruby cried.

"It's miracle!" PohPoh cried.

And it was. Flying Duck had saved Oscar's life.

"*Waaaaaaaaaah!*" Oscar screamed. He turned pink.

Owowowowowow! The sirens screamed outside.

Lights flashed. It was the most exciting afternoon of Ruby's life. A small crowd had gathered on the sidewalk. The ambulance people were racing up the front steps to her house, just like on TV.

"Wow," Ruby said. Then she realized that none of these marvelous things would be happening if Flying Duck hadn't come from

China. Her breath made a little cloud on the front window, where she stood watching the excitement with Flying Duck.

The entire afternoon would have been boring without her cousin.

Ruby's life would be boring.

Ruby blinked.

Then she looked at Flying Duck. Her cousin was breathing on the window too. Between the two of them, there were quite a number of clouds, perfect for writing in.

"Flying Duck," Ruby said, spelling out her cousin's name in one of the clouds.

"Look, Flying Duck," she said, pointing to her writing on the window.

Aw-some

Talented

Magnifeecent

Frendly

Helpful

Happy

Wunderful

Humbul

No. 1 cousin

Some girl

Ruby stepped back to admire her work. She took a deep breath.

"Thanks for saving Oscar's life," Ruby finally said, remembering to wiggle her thumbs.

"And thanks for being here," she added, giving Flying Duck a big hug.

Suddenly immigration wasn't quite so miserable anymore. Ruby's mother had been right. It didn't even seem so scary.

But was it *ever* going to get easier?

Ruby blinked.

What if it didn't? What if it *never* got easier?

Ruby swallowed.

It didn't matter, she decided. For the first time since Flying Duck arrived, Ruby felt like her cousin belonged right where she was.

3

Deaf Is Not a Disadvantage

Being a Smile Buddy was a big responsibility.

Ruby kept her room a little neater.

She brushed her hair, regularly.

She flossed her teeth.

She ate her Brussels sprouts.

She was nice to her brother, mostly.

She wore her Smile Buddy pin, always.

And for the first time ever, Ruby worked diligently at her Chinese school homework.

She studied her characters.

She practiced her vocabulary.

She listened to her tapes.

She even made a little ink and gave her brush a little workout.

"A miracle," Ruby's mother said. "A true miracle."

Ruby beamed. Learning Chinese was not easy. It took a lot of concentration. But slowly—and with Flying Duck's help—Ruby began to understand her cousin and her aunt and uncle a little better.

Ruby could hardly be more responsible. But she was.

At school Ruby became a dispenser of valuable information. She stood up at the beginning of Reading Carpet Time and made a speech.

"Never sneak up on a deaf person," Ruby said. Her voice wobbled just a little, but mostly it was firm, like Jell-O. Making a speech was a little scary. "Get her attention first by calling her name or waving."

It was a helpful idea. Everyone sat up and listened.

The next day Ruby made another speech. "Look a deaf person smack in the eye"—she demonstrated—"before you speak."

The class was riveted.

"If you don't understand each other, write it out," Ruby said in another speech.

"If she doesn't understand you, say it differently," she added the day after that.

Ruby's observations were keen and insightful.

Even Ruby's teacher, Mr. Tupahotu, was impressed. So Ruby's Tips and Helpful Hints became a daily fixture at the beginning of Reading Carpet Time.

"Deaf is not a disadvantage. The only thing a deaf person can't do is hear."

"Speak clearly and do not exaggerate mouth movements."

"Do not chew gum."

Flying Duck nodded. Gum chewing made lip-reading impossible.

Then came Ruby's most important speech of all:

"After repeating yourself twenty times, never say, 'Forget it, it's not important.'"

Ruby puffed out her chest. Her Smile Buddy pin shimmered just so. Ruby beamed.

Ruby's latest speech was so important that Mr. Tupahotu wrote it on the board. In cursive.

It was very impressive.

But that was not all.

One day Ruby got picked for the most responsible task of all.

She got to take Flying Duck to the nurse's office for her eye test.

Usually children at Kimball Elementary got their eyes tested in the fall. That way, if you needed glasses, you could have them for the whole year. But because Flying Duck didn't emigrate until spring break, she didn't get an eye test until it was nearly the end of the school year.

Ruby could hardly believe her luck.

Ruby loved the eye test. In fact, she had a copy of it taped to the ceiling above her bed. At night she often fell asleep practicing it through one eye or another, just as a musician might practice a piece of music. She knew that she'd have to make it all the way to the end of the chart perfectly to get glasses. And she had wanted glasses ever since she could remember.

But no matter how much she practiced, every year the nurse would stop Ruby at the end of the same line, and her turn would be over. And the next person in line would step up and begin to read. But now there would be no line . . . Maybe the nurse wouldn't be in such a hurry. Maybe it was Ruby's lucky day!

"I-W-T-M-Y," Flying Duck read with one eye covered.

Ruby gasped.

Whenever Flying Duck spoke English, it

always came out wrong. Mostly it sounded like Chinese. But Ruby was used to hearing English like that. And she could make it sound like English.

"T-V-I-N-P!" Ruby translated for her.

"F-V-D-B-G!" Flying Duck said, covering her other eye.

"A-P-E-O-D!" Ruby translated again. Flying Duck had gotten it all wrong!

The school nurse stopped. She looked at Ruby. Then she looked at Flying Duck.

"She can't read English too well, even with both eyes open," Ruby said. "So I have to translate for her."

"Oh?" said Miss Wong, the nurse.

"I can read anything with just one eye," Ruby added proudly, covering one eye. She demonstrated.

"How about this?" Miss Wong pointed to a smaller line.

"B-T-S-O-A!" Ruby recited excitedly.

Miss Wong scribbled on her notepad.

"Try this." Miss Wong pointed to a barely visible line.

Ruby squinted really hard. She could hardly believe it. Miss Wong was giving her the eye test too!

"D-Q-C-O-F!" Ruby said from memory.

"Hmmm," said Miss Wong. She made another note.

Ruby had to think fast. It was her last chance at glasses until next fall. She was so close, she could almost feel a little plastic frame resting on the bridge of her nose. So

she squeezed both eyes shut and blurted out the last two lines on the chart, letter for letter, just like that.

When she opened her eyes, Miss Wong's eyes were wide open too.

It was the first time Ruby ever got through the whole eye test.

Maybe it was even the first time anyone tried it with their eyes *closed*.

It was very impressive.

But that was not all.

When Ruby and Flying Duck got back to class . . .

A letter arrived.

RUBY LU, ROOM 11, it said in fancy letters. The envelope was bright red. Mr. Tupahotu set it on Ruby's desk with a smile.

"Open it when you get home," he said.

The entire class turned and stared. Mr. Tupahotu had no more red envelopes to hand out. So naturally Ruby thought she was busted, and so did everyone else. Letters handed out by teachers are scary in that way. They make you jittery. And Ruby was not unfamiliar with scary letters or the jitters.

So naturally it was very difficult for Ruby not to peek. She waited as long as she could (about five seconds) . . . and then . . . when Mr. Tupahotu turned his back to the class, Ruby made her move.

Dear Smile Buddy, the letter began in beautiful curlicue letters. *Being a Smile Buddy is a big responsibility.* It took Ruby's breath away.

Nothing could be more exciting, the letter continued.

Ruby's mouth opened in surprise. It was as if the letter were repeating her thoughts!

"Are you busted?" whispered Tiger, who was sitting next to Ruby.

Ruby ignored him.

"Please open your books to page thirty-eight," said Mr. Tupahotu from the front of the room.

Ruby ignored him, too.

She slipped the letter between the pages of her book. She read on breathlessly. Her fingers guided her eyes slowly but steadily across the words.

Thank you for being a Smile Buddy this year, Ruby continued silently, carefully stringing each word like macaroni on a necklace. *You've helped someone feel welcome.*

"Ruby, would you please read for us, beginning at the top of the page?" Mr. Tupahotu asked.

Ruby was a very good reader. Her eyes could move ahead of her lips so that she could see what words were coming before

they fell out of her
mouth. She had learned to do this by
the end of first grade. So that now, near the
end of second grade, she could roll at a

pretty good clip. In fact, she could read so well that whenever she got started, she couldn't stop until she'd run out of words. And often she was asked to read first, to set the rhythm and pace for the rest of the class.

"This has been an awesome year for Smile Buddies," Ruby read, loud and clear. "You and your buddy are invited to the annual Smile Buddy Tea."

Wow. It was a dream come true! Ruby could hardly believe her eyes.

"Please bring ten dollars and a dessert," Ruby read excitedly. "The ten dollars will pay for T-shirts for you and your buddy. You will get to meet other buddies. There will be a fun activity. Please do not forget your ten dollars and dessert, or you and your buddy will be without a shirt and dessert. See you there, with both ten dollars and a dessert! Sincerely, The Smile Buddy Committee.

"P.S. Don't forget to bring your buddy." Ruby finally ran out of words. She looked up.

The class split open like a great big watermelon. Laughter dripped everywhere.

Oops. Ruby had read from the top of the page, but it was not the page of her textbook—it was her red letter!

"Ruby, please bring me that letter," Mr. Tupahotu said. Usually he praised Ruby for her reading ability. But not this time.

Ruby was busted. She wished she were a pigeon and could fly out the window with her letter. But she couldn't. She got up slowly from her desk.

"I will keep this for you," her teacher said.

Then the red envelope with the matching

red letter disappeared into Mr. Tupahotu's desk drawer.

Ruby's stomach nearly lurched into the drawer too.

She wanted to cry.

It was Ruby's first fancy invitation with her name on it. And just like that, it was gone.

"Don't worry," Wally whispered. "He'll probably give it back to you at the end of the day."

But Ruby was worried. Anything could happen.

Her invitation could get thrown out with desk junk.

The school might burn down.

The world might end.

Or worse, Mr. Tupahotu might forget about it completely.

Ruby crossed her fingers and held her breath.

At lunch she made a wish upon her turkey tofu pup.

At recess she consulted her origami fortune-teller.

As a last resort she sent her teacher mind-controlling stares from across the room, several times.

But nothing worked.

Ruby felt terrible.

But at the end of the day—surprise, surprise—Ruby's wishes and hocus-pocus began to work! Mr. Tupahotu opened his drawer . . . and pulled out . . . a letter . . . and pinned it . . . to Flying Duck's sweater.

Ruby's mouth opened in surprise. She could hardly believe her eyes. She squinted, just to be sure.

But before Ruby had a chance to remind him that he might have something in there for her, he pulled out an identical envelope and pinned it to Ruby's sweater!

But it was not the right letter.

The envelope was sealed.

It was addressed to *The Parents of . . .*

It was the wrong color. These letters were not invitation red at all. They were official, you-are-so-busted white.

Worse, no one else got a letter. This was not a good sign.

"*Iorana korua*," Mr. Tupahotu said. He always said good-bye in Rapa Nui.

"*Iorana koe*," everyone replied.

Everyone, that is, except Ruby.

Ruby was speechless.

The Earth stopped.

The sun went out.

Worst of all, when Ruby reached to adjust her World's Best Smile Buddy pin, she couldn't. The letter was fastened in such a way that it covered her pin totally and completely, just like a full solar eclipse.

4

How to Feel Like a Winner

Pinned letters cast a terrifying spell. They loom large. They make you forget everything else.

Flying Duck had no idea what a pinned letter meant.

But Ruby did.

Report cards are pinned.

Homework notices are pinned.

News about getting shots is pinned.

News about getting busted is pinned.

Ruby had had many letters pinned to her sweater. It was never good news. In fact, it was always bad news. Really *important* bad news.

To make matters even worse, someone who was good at guessing could usually figure out exactly what a pinned letter said.

"You two are *so* busted," Christina said. Christina was a bully when she first moved to 20th Avenue South. For a while she looked like a strange bird after school, her many pinned letters flapping like feathers, she was that bad. So she knew all about being busted.

"But we didn't do anything wrong," Ruby said.

"Then why would you get busted?" Wally asked.

Ruby shrugged.

"Think hard," Tiger urged.

Ruby could not think hard. She could hardly think at all.

"Have you been doing your homework?" Christina asked.

"Most of the time," Ruby said. "Well . . . sort of." She hesitated. "But I do Flying Duck's!"

"Then you should be getting a star, not a letter," Wally said, scratching his head.

"Have you been in a fight?"

"No."

"Did you return your library books?"

"Yes."

"Did you pick up your summer reading list?"

"I think so."

"Wait a minute . . . ," Tiger began, "if you've only been 'sort of' doing your homework . . . and you've been doing Flying Duck's, that

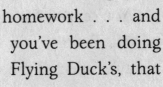

means that she isn't doing her work at all, and you're not doing yours, right?"

Ruby leaned to one side, then to the other. Her yoga leg stretched up, then it came down. Finally she nodded.

"This could mean only one thing, then," Tiger concluded. "You're both flunking out!"

Ruby let out a little cry, but clapped her hand over her mouth. Flunking out ran in her family. Her father was a Chinese school FOB. Her mother repeated citizenship class three times. And Ruby herself had nearly flunked kindergarten.

"You're pan-fried noodle," Emma whispered. Emma was a little anxious and always expected the worst.

But not Christina. Christina was from California. She expected sunshine even when it was thunderstorms with a chance of electrocution.

"They can't flunk you if your parents don't sign the letter," she said.

Ruby took a deep breath. A good Smile Buddy was always prepared.

So halfway between school and home, where there were no grown-ups, and where all sorts of trouble begin, Ruby unpinned her letter.

Everyone gasped.

Then she unpinned the letter from Flying Duck's sweater.

Everyone watched in silent awe.

Then she put the letters in her backpack. Way down at the bottom of her backpack.

It was the most daring thing anyone on 20th Avenue South had ever done. Pinned letters are supposed to be unpinned only by

a grown-up. It is the law.

"In the face of uncertainty, maintain your dignity," Ruby said bravely. There was only a slight quiver in her voice. Ruby had heard her father say that whenever he was about to lose at Scrabble. Ruby didn't know what it meant, but somehow she felt it was appropriate.

Maybe it had something to do with feeling like a winner even when you're a loser.

Ruby felt more like a winner with no letter pinned to her sweater.

And she thought Flying Duck looked better too.

It was definitely more . . . dignified.

Then she put her arm around her cousin.

And they went home.

5

So Busted!

Hiding the letters was the perfect alternative to flunking out.

Ruby's parents didn't see them.

Nothing got signed.

Nothing changed.

After a while Ruby's friends forgot about the letters.

Even Ruby herself hardly remembered them at all.

"Out of sight, out of mind," Ruby's father often said. Ruby loved that saying. It meant that if he'd hidden something, he'd never think of it again.

There was only one little problem.

Emma.

Emma was Ruby's next-door neighbor.

And Emma never forgot anything.

She and Ruby were best friends, sometimes. They both had baby brothers, Sam and Oscar, who were best buds. And Emma had a funny little dog, Elwyn, who had a mouthful of pointy teeth and little feet with toenails that went *dop-dop-dop* wherever he went.

Elwyn was the first friend that Flying Duck made in the neighborhood. He was curious about everything new or different. When Flying Duck first arrived, he sniffed her. Then he licked her. Then he played ball with her. After that they were friends.

But Emma was not like her dog. She didn't like anything new or different. She liked

everything to be the same. To
make matters worse, Emma had
heard that Flying Duck was
not an American citizen,
she was called an "alien."
Emma knew all about
aliens. They were creatures
from outer space. Their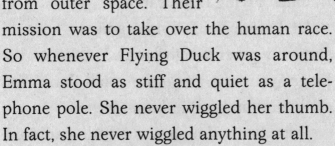
mission was to take over the human race.
So whenever Flying Duck was around,
Emma stood as stiff and quiet as a telephone pole. She never wiggled her thumb.
In fact, she never wiggled anything at all.

"Emma just needs more time to adjust,"
Ruby's mother had told Ruby. "Just be your-
selves and she'll come around."

Emma came around all right.

"Did your parents see the letter yet?" Emma
asked nervously. It was morning recess.

"What letter?" Ruby stopped.

"The one that says you're flunking second grade," Emma said.

Ruby froze.

Uh-oh. That letter. Ruby had nearly completely forgotten about that letter. She shook her head.

"I didn't think so," Emma said. She watched Flying Duck carefully.

"If I were you," Emma added, "I would show my parents right away. You know, the longer you wait, the more you'll flunk. You could end up back in kindergarten."

Ruby knew Emma was a little paranoid. But sometimes Emma was right. Before Ruby had a chance to think about it for too long, Emma had something else to say.

"You know about aliens, right?" Emma whispered. "You know not to play with one if you saw one, right?"

Ruby blinked. She glanced at Flying

Duck. Ruby, too, had heard that her cousin was an alien. But she was not afraid of them. Her mother was an alien before she learned to be an ordinary person in citizenship classes. So Ruby was actually quite proud that aliens ran in her family. She only wished that she had been born an alien too.

"You're just jealous, Emma Jean!" Ruby cried.

"Am not!"

"Are too!"

"Am not!"

Flying Duck didn't understand the commotion, but she had something to say to Emma.

"Pay me!" Flying Duck said in her best English. "Pay me!"

Flying Duck's English was not perfect. She had meant to say, "Play with me," but it came out wrong.

Emma frowned.

She twisted her hair.

She narrowed her eyes.

Then Emma cracked.

"Save yourself!" she screamed at Ruby.

Ruby gasped.

"She's an alien!" Emma pointed at Flying Duck. "She's come to snatch us all away and use us in medical experiments! And she's already got you in her clutches!"

Games stopped. A tetherball hit someone in the head. Hopscotch markers dropped. It

was only morning recess. Usually nothing unusual happened during morning recess—only during afternoon recess.

Suddenly Flying Duck didn't feel so good. She ran off the playground and headed straight to the nurse's office.

And Emma headed to the principal's office for a time-out.

Then Ruby tried to jump Emma, who was on her way to the principal's office.

But the playground monitor caught her midjump.

That night, for the first time since Flying Duck and her family arrived, it was quiet at Ruby's house.

Nobody knew what to say.

Nobody knew what to do.

The principal's secretary had called and spoken to Ruby's mother. Getting a phone call was worse than getting twenty-five hundred pinned letters.

Ruby had worked so hard to help Flying Duck feel at home in her new country, and to do better in school, but now everything was ruined.

Worst of all, their parents were scheduled for an emergency meeting with the principal.

Ruby was as busted as a can of beans under the tire of a truck.

She was one dead bean.

Ruby's lips turned down. A tear ran down one cheek. Then a tear ran down the other cheek.

"EmmasaidthatFlyingDuckwasanalien andthatshehadcometosnatchusallawayfor experimentssoItriedtojumpheronherway totheprincipal'soffice," Ruby confessed all at once.

She came up for breath.

"And I'm sorry I tried to jump her," Ruby cried. Then she ran into her mother's arms and burst into thunderous sobs.

6

The Principal's Office

This is how to say you're sorry in Chinese Sign Language: Salute the person to whom you are apologizing with your left hand. Then touch your left pinky finger to your chest over and over again.

Emma had asked Flying Duck's mother to teach her to apologize.

Then she practiced all weekend.

Then she surprised Flying Duck.

She said she was sorry in perfect sign first thing Monday morning.

Then it was Ruby's turn. Ruby did not like to apologize.

But she was in the principal's office.

She stood on one foot. Then she stood on the other. Then she glanced around the room, three whole times.

Finally Ruby said she was sorry (in a little voice) for having tried to jump Emma . . . even though Emma deserved it (in a louder voice).

Then Emma got to go back to class, she was so lucky. And Ruby's and Flying Duck's parents got called in from the waiting room.

Miss Kallianpur, the principal, gave this report on Ruby:

Ruby had been a "fine example" to the entire school of how to welcome someone new. She had been a wonderful Smile Buddy.

"I am very proud of Ruby," she said. "Helping someone adjust to a new country is not easy."

But . . .

Not only did Ruby forget her playground manners . . .

Her work was suffering. Her book reports, which used to be as thick as Russian novels, were now as thin as a passport application.

In geography she'd said that the second-longest river in the United States is the Yangtze. (It is not. The second-longest river in the USA is the Mississippi River, which runs 2,340 miles.)

In history she'd said that George Washington was the first emperor of the United States. (He was not.)

And her math, which was never her best subject anyway, was now completely and totally incomprehensible.

In other words, Ruby was a full-time Smile Buddy, and a no-time student.

As for Flying Duck, the report on her was as follows:

All of her ESL homework had been neatly and correctly done.

Her book reports were as thick as Russian novels. And her handwriting on all her homework looked oddly identical to Ruby's.

Did anyone know anything about that?

"Rubeee . . . ," Ruby's father began. He glowed like a red-hot coal.

Ruby was really busted now.

"It's been a disruptive year for both of them," Miss Kallianpur said. "I was a bit confused too when I first came to this country." She herself had come from India when she was Ruby and Flying Duck's age.

"Flying Duck needs more time to adjust to her new surroundings," Miss

Kallianpur continued. "And Ruby . . . well, Ruby needs to adjust to her new circumstances too."

So it was decided, on the brink of summer break, that both Flying Duck and Ruby . . . would attend summer school.

"A little extra help will do wonders for them," Miss Kallianpur said.

Ruby's parents agreed, and so did Flying Duck's. Summer school was a great idea. Ruby had been to summer school once before and had learned more in summer school than she had her entire kindergarten year.

"A miracle," Ruby's mother had said back then. "A true miracle."

And it had been. Ruby was famous when she showed up in first grade. On her sweater was a big blue ribbon from summer school and in shiny gold letters it said,

GENIUS. No one else had on such a ribbon. No one in first grade could even read it. No one, that is, except for Ruby.

But things are different when you're nearly eight.

Ruby had summer plans.

Big plans.

And these did not include summer school.

That night it was hard to fall asleep.

Ruby's and Flying Duck's eyes were as large as lychee fruits.

The stars moved across the night window from their spring positions to their summer ones, but neither Ruby nor Flying Duck noticed.

And Ruby's backpack, the one containing the unpinned letters, was set in its summer position too, in the back of Ruby's closet.

Ruby blinked.

For a moment she remembered the letters. They were never mentioned in the principal's office. Not once. Not even a hint. It was odd. But it was a miracle. Suddenly the prospect of summer school didn't seem so bad. They had been busted for not doing their work, but at least they hadn't *flunked*. It was a very close call.

Then the memory of those letters led to the memory of another one.

Oh no! Ruby had completely forgotten

about her invitation to the tea! She and Flying Duck had missed the tea altogether! But Ruby was too tired to feel too terrible about it. Summer was now just a wink away.

7

The Trouble with Swimming Lessons

The first day of the summer holiday changes everything.

Even with the looming threat of summer school.

Even with the dismal history of second grade.

Even with the difficulties of immigration.

Everything looks different.

Doors bang.

Windows open.

Flowers look expectantly upward.

A fly pings off a metal garbage can.

Somewhere a gate yawns and closes.

And somewhere else, a car blows its nose.

Honk!

Flying Duck's parents were still job hunting.

They clipped job ads from the Chinese newspaper.

They made phone calls.

They filled out applications.

Ruby's father tutored them in interviewing skills. And Ruby's mother gave them tips and helpful hints on proper dress and etiquette.

"No white socks," Ruby's mother instructed. "Smile and shake hands."

Purpose brimmed from every heart, especially Ruby's.

She made a list:

My 12-Step Summer ~~Gols Gaols~~ Plans:
1. Hold breth in swiming skool.

2. put face in water.*
3. Blo bubels.*
4. Be frends again with Emma.*
5. Play with Flying Duck.
6. Play with Oscar.

Reluctantly she added:

7. Go to summer skool.*
*maybe

It wasn't exactly twelve steps, but it was close. Still, something was missing from her list. What was it? Ruby could not quite put her knuckle on it . . . it was something very important . . . but Ruby just couldn't concentrate.

"C'mon, Flying Duck," she said, giving up on remembering. And they both ran outside.

The sidewalk was sizzling. The grass was

roasting. The sun burned brighter and hotter than a million tiki torches.

Ruby's neighborhood buddies were already wedged in the branches of her plum tree. And the tree was abuzz. It was the first

summer meeting of the 20th Avenue South Plum Club. And everyone was talking about the rumor that Ruby and Flying Duck were headed to summer school.

"It's not a rumor," Ruby said glumly.

Everyone was stunned. Even Elwyn howled his dismay.

Ruby was the president of the Plum Club because the tree was in her backyard. Everyone else was a member. Membership was open to anyone who lived on 20th Avenue South, but it was okay if you lived on 19th Avenue South or even 23rd Avenue South. Members included anyone who could climb the plum tree, but it was okay if you could not (Oscar and Sam), or would not (Emma was afraid of heights). The Plum Club met whenever there was anything to talk about or for no reason at all.

"You might as well be going to jail," Wally said.

Wally was right. Summer was for running through the sprinkler and chasing the ice-cream truck.

Summer was for sitting in the plum tree.

And doing science experiments on the sidewalk.

Summer was for doing everything. And doing nothing.

But summer was definitely *not* for summer school.

Everyone felt sorry for Ruby and Flying Duck.

Everyone, that is, except Emma.

"I never needed the extra help," she snorted.

"Summer school is actually . . . kind of *fun*," Ruby said, trying to remember her earlier summer school experience. "It's like . . . going to *camp*."

"Really?" said Emma.

"Yup," Ruby said. "*Better* than camp. You get extra help and extra snacks. You get extra, extra, extra everything!"

"Ruby Lu!" Emma steamed. "You're just trying to make me jealous."

"Am not!"

"Are too!"

"Am not!"

"Everyone knows that summer school is for dummies!" Emma blurted.

Ruby gasped. She could hardly stand it. Some days she and Emma were best friends. But other days Ruby could just . . .

"Rubeeeeee!" It was Ruby's mother. She was on the back step with Oscar on her hip. "Time for your swim lesson!"

Oh no! Ruby had spent the entire last summer at the pool and did not once put her face in. This summer she especially dreaded swim school because Flying Duck could hold her breath for forty-two seconds, no problem.

"Beeeee!" Oscar waved.

Oscar was in his swimsuit. He could hardly wait. But Ruby was allergic to water. Ruby wondered how Oscar found his swim-suit after she had hidden it so well.

So Ruby did not answer her mother or Oscar.

But Emma's mother did.

"What a good idea!" Emma's mom called from the next yard. She was hanging out wash. "Why don't we take *all* the kids? I'll give the other moms a call."

That afternoon Ruby, president of the Plum Club, and her entire *presidential* entourage ended up in the pool.

Oscar and Sam dove straight into the water babies' class.

Wally, Tiger, and Flying Duck, who possessed unnatural breath-holding abilities, moved into Coral Cay.

Christina jumped right into Motorboat Lane. She had lived in California before she moved to 20th Avenue South and was an excellent swimmer. She had been to the beach. She had floated in the ocean. She had gotten her face wet. She had even gotten sand in her bathing suit.

But poor Emma. She disliked the

water even more than
Ruby. Ruby was aqua-
phobic and had flunked
out of swim school
three summers in a
row. Emma, who was
also aquaphobic, had

managed to avoid swim lessons altogether.
Until now.

She was strapped into personal flotation
devices (PFDs) from eyebrow to anklebone.
Just like Ruby.

And they both ended up in Shallow
Shores.

"What's shallow?" Emma peeped, looking at the water.

"Don't know," Ruby squeaked.

They climbed in.

The water licked their chins. It was very
scary.

"Honey, if you're going to pray, don't worry," Ruby advised Emma just before chomping down on her own breathing tube. "And if you're going to worry, don't pray." Ruby had heard this on the bus, where there was always lots of good advice.

Emma shivered. Goose bumps covered her little arms. She looked straight ahead. She breathed heavily through her tube.

Ruby breathed heavily too. She pretended she was a water frog, but it was no use. She was not pond or pool compatible. She thought of only one thing: drowning. Nothing could be more dreadful. Except maybe drowning in Shallow Shores in front of her friends while wearing her PFDs.

Ruby clung for dear life to the side of the pool. So did Emma.

Meanwhile the rest of the class bobbed up and down like mermaids and mermen and blew bubbles until the pool looked like soda.

"I remember you from last summer!" said Danny, the swim instructor, squirting a stream of water through his hands at Ruby. It was a lifeguard trick that usually made swimmers squeal with delight.

"Ur e-em-er-ur oo," Ruby said through her tube. She remembered him, too.

"I was hoping you'd be back!" he said cheerfully.

"Oo er?" Ruby's tube said.

"Of course I was!" Danny said. "I wanted you to come back so I could teach you to swim like a shark.

"I see you brought a friend!" Danny pointed to Emma. "Good for you!"

"I am ot er en," Emma mumbled through her tube.

Ruby gasped.

"You're not her friend?" Danny repeated.

He was fluent in air tube. "Well, I'm sure you'll be friends by the time the summer is over."

Emma's face mask fogged over.

Ruby felt the same way about Emma. She could hardly stand clinging to the same section of wall. They were two enemy barnacles, each stuck with the other, unable to move away.

It was going to be a long, soggy summer.

8

A Regular Lifeguard

"The first sign of a drowning person is flailing arms. . . ."

Ruby gasped. She was watching a video from the library, *Basic Lifesaving*. Ruby's father had taken her to the library and did not do the usual inspection of Ruby's selections the way her mother did. Ruby stared at the flailing arms. She wondered why someone would film a drowning person instead of saving him.

"Bee! Bee!" Oscar shouted excitedly, pointing at the screen. "You, Bee?"

"A drowning person makes no noise or calls for help," the narrator droned. "So you must watch for signs."

Ruby could not drag her eyes away.

"Oh," said Oscar. He sounded like a little owl in a tree.

Oscar was in his swimsuit.

And so was Flying Duck.

But Ruby was not.

"C'mon, Ruby," Ruby's father called, scooping Oscar into his arms and carrying him out to the car. "We're already late!"

Ruby's mother had taken Flying Duck's parents to job interviews. So Ruby's father was in charge.

"I'm coming!" Ruby called back.

But she was not. She ran into her room to look for her swimsuit.

It was not under her bed.

It was not behind her bookcase.

It was not among her rock collection.

It was not even under her magic carpet, where other things had been known to mysteriously appear and disappear.

And it was not in the UtterPrincess box, which had never been opened. . . .

Slowly and carefully, Ruby lifted UtterPrincess out of her box for the very first time ever. Ruby had saved her doll in the original box for as long as she could stand. Unopened dolls were "collectible," Christina had told her. But anyone could see that UtterPrincess was utterly useless in her box. All she collected was dust. But outside the box . . . UtterPrincess was utterly awesome. Ruby turned her around five whole times to see her from every angle.

"Ruby!" Ruby's father shouted. "Move yourself down to the car, before I move you myself!"

Before Ruby knew it, her father had tucked her under his arm and was heading out the door.

"But, Dad!" Ruby cried. "I can't leave her out!"

Ruby's father had no idea what Ruby was talking about. He was as patient as a hot iron on a no-iron shirt.

Ruby was stunned. Her eyes grew big and round. Her mouth formed an *O*. But nothing

came out. Not a sound. She was completely and totally horrified.

UtterPrincess was still in her hand.

The pool looked murderous.

The waves were bigger than usual.

Oscar and Sam were making tsunami noises in the water babies' corner.

Ruby's aquaphobia was worse than ever. When her father carried her out of the house, there was no time to get her mask, her nose plugs and earplugs, or water wings or life jacket or breathing tube. This was the first time in her life that Ruby was without her PFDs. She was even without her swimsuit— she was wearing a T-shirt and shorts!

It had been a week since swim school began, and suddenly everything at the pool looked so different. Danny, the swim instructor, was as brown as a cookie freckled with a billion chocolate chips. Wally, Tiger, and Christina swam back and forth like porpoises. And Flying Duck glided peacefully through the water like a frog.

Only one thing hadn't changed.

Emma.

Emma was clinging to the side of the pool for dear life. She breathed heavily through her tube. And her diving mask was totally fogged.

"Emma!" Ruby cried, forgetting that they weren't friends.

But Emma only shivered.

Ruby slipped in and grabbed the side of the pool next to Emma. Dragon-boat drums pounded in Ruby's ears. *Doom, doom-da-doom-doom-doom!*

Basic Lifesaving played in her head. "The first sign of a drowning person is flailing arms. . . ."

"Your turn!" called a cheerful voice.

Ruby jumped.

It was Danny, and he was smiling at Ruby.

"C'mon, little mermaid," he said, sprinkling a little water on Ruby's head. Ruby liked Danny, but she didn't like his habit of sprinkling.

"Blow big bubbles for me," he said.

Ruby put her lips together and blew. She blew and blew and blew. But there were no bubbles. Her lips were nowhere near the water.

"Who's this?" Danny asked. "Bring another little friend?"

Ruby turned her head stiffly and swiveled her eyes to where Danny was pointing.

"Oh no!" she cried. She had brought UtterPrincess into the pool! And she was holding her underwater!

"Hey, that's UtterPrincess!" Danny exclaimed.

"Oh no!" Ruby cried again. Her doll was totally and completely ruined!

"That's no ordinary doll," Danny said. "That's the action figure that swims and skates and knows five languages!"

Ruby's mouth dropped open. *Action figure?* How did Danny know?

"I used to have UtterLord," he said. "He was the coolest.

"Want to see her swim, Ruby?" Danny said. Danny held out his hand for UtterPrincess. But Ruby didn't move. She was as stiff as a chopstick. So Danny had to reach underwater to loosen UtterPrincess from Ruby's utter grip.

"See?" he said, gently setting Ruby's doll on top of the water. UtterPrincess, still in her clothes, began kicking her legs and moving through the water. Ruby could not believe her eyes.

"Wow," was all Ruby could say when Danny gave UtterPrincess back to her.

"She looks like you," Danny said. "You can swim like that, too."

"Can't," Ruby said.

"You mean 'won't,'" Danny said.

"Okay, won't," Ruby said. "And you can't make me."

Danny laughed. "Look, you're not even holding on to the wall anymore!"

Ruby froze. She looked around. Danny was right. She was not even anywhere near the wall. Somehow she had drifted with Danny into the middle of the pool. All of a sudden she didn't feel so good.

"C'mon," Danny said, leading her back to the side of the pool where Emma was clinging and watching.

Ruby clutched the edge with one hand and UtterPrincess with the other.

"Hi, Emma!" Ruby said, forgetting again that they hadn't made up. Emma looked at Ruby out of the corner of her eye.

Emma was holding her breath. Then she did something completely and utterly unexpected.

She put her face in. For a split fraction of a split second.

But Ruby saw it. And so did Danny.

"Good!" Danny exclaimed as Emma came up gasping like a scary monster.

"Now it's your turn!" Danny turned to Ruby.

"No," said Ruby firmly.

Ruby would never put her face in. A wet face led to flailing arms. And flailing arms led to . . . to . . . Ruby couldn't bring herself to say it.

"Well, maybe your friend here will get you to do it," Danny said, pointing to Emma. Then he began to help the other swimmers.

"I am ot er en," Emma managed through her tube.

Ruby swallowed hard and blinked back tears. She could hardly believe that Emma would say that *again.*

Then she gently set UtterPrincess on top of the water. The waves were not so big after all. Ruby held on to the wall with one hand as she watched UtterPrincess glide through the water. First on her back, then with her face in the water. But to really play with her *action figure*, Ruby needed to let go of the wall. If she didn't let go, she could lose UtterPrincess. The utter action figure was already swimming away. So, reluctantly, Ruby let go, one finger at a time.

Suddenly she felt like a piece of drift-wood in the sea. It was scary.

But it was also exciting. Ruby smiled just a little. Then she smiled a little more. Then she grabbed the wall again.

For the first time, she didn't mind the water so much. She waved to her father. Her father waved back. Then, without thinking about it, Ruby let go of the wall again. And slowly she drifted on tiptoe away from the wall, just as she had done earlier when Danny was talking to her.

Now she could play with UtterPrincess.

Suddenly it happened!

The flailing arms!

Ruby gasped.

Over near the wall where Emma had been standing, there was wild splashing and— flailing arms. Just like the ones in *Basic Lifesaving*.

"A drowning person makes no noise . . . or calls for help," the voice droned in Ruby's head.

Before Ruby could help it, her face was in the water. The water was cool, but Ruby didn't notice. And Ruby didn't notice her legs either—they were kicking like crazy.

Ruby's heart pounded inside her little chest. She didn't know what she was doing, but she had to do it fast. She couldn't hold her breath for forty-two seconds like Flying Duck. She couldn't even hold it for two.

"Identify yourself and announce your intention in a loud voice," the narrator droned in Ruby's ears.

"Lifeguard here!" Ruby gurgled. "I'll take you to safety!"

She swallowed water. Something burned inside her nose. She reached out and grabbed Emma around the middle. "Use the cross-chest carry," the narrator's voice droned on. Ruby pulled her to the wall.

Everything stopped.

Emma coughed and coughed. She turned thunderstorm gray. Then purple mountains'

majesty. Then bruised peach. Then she started to cry.

Ruby coughed too, just a little. And she wanted to cry, too. Drums pounded loudly in her ears.

"What happened?" All the swimmers surrounded them and wanted to know.

"Emma just swallowed a little water," Danny said reassuringly. "She's okay." Then he winked at Ruby.

"I knew it all along," Danny said to Ruby. "You're a regular lifeguard!"

Ruby's teeth clattered like castanets. She didn't know what to say. She actually didn't know how to swim at all. She had never even put her face in the water before. All Ruby did was what *Basic Lifesaving* told her. Now suddenly she felt very tired.

Emma's babysitter wrapped Emma in a towel and took her away.

Ruby's father wrapped Ruby, Flying Duck, and Oscar in towels and took them away, too.

Then everyone else went home. Everyone, that is, except UtterPrincess.

UtterPrincess was still kicking around the pool.

But the pool didn't look so murderous anymore. It didn't even look like soda.

9

All About Summer School

Ruby was a hero.

She had been very brave.

She went back to the pool.

She held her breath again. She kicked her legs. She blew bubbles. Then she put her face in . . . and *floated*.

Soon she passed her swim test.

She got her first swim badge. It was not as big as her Smile Buddy pin, but it was just as important. She sewed it on to her orange swimsuit with a little help from her mother, but mostly all by herself.

Then Ruby crossed off her list:

~~1. Hold breth in swiming skool.~~
~~2. Put face in water.~~*
~~3. Blo bubels.~~*

Wow. Summer could hardly get any better.

But it did.

Emma came over.

Emma did not pass her swim test, but she had made a special card for Ruby.

Thank you, it said. There was a drawing of Ruby and Emma in the pool. The water licked their chins. But they were smiling. And nothing about it was scary. Inside the card Emma had written *Thank you* one hundred times in her best handwriting. She handed it to Ruby and gave her a big hug. And they were friends again, just like that.

Then—surprise, surprise—Emma wiggled her thumbs at Flying Duck.

So Flying Duck invited Emma to stay for a milk shake. A special summer sidewalk milk shake. Emma had seen these before. She took off her sandals and stood as still as she could. Then Flying Duck poured a vanilla milk shake on Emma's bare feet.

"Good?" Flying Duck asked.

"Perfect," Emma purred. "Just perfect."

And it was. Everything about summer was just perfect.

Well, almost everything. Ruby and Flying Duck still had to go to summer school.

. . .

In summer school the windows were always wide open.

Breezes blew in. Papers swirled about.

Sometimes birds flew in.

Sometimes they flew out.

When a hornet landed on Ruby's desk, everyone screamed hysterically and ran. Desks overturned. Chairs toppled. Ruby screamed the most hysterically of all and ran the fastest. It was the best pandemonium in summer school history.

The playground was interesting, too.

The slide was as hot as a wok on blue flames.

"Owwwww!" Flying Duck cried, rubbing her roasted legs.

"It's a regular barbecue!" Ruby screamed.

Flying Duck looked at Ruby. And Ruby looked at Flying Duck. Without a word, they both knew . . . it was just perfect for . . .

Frying an egg!

The next day Ruby snuck in an egg. Flying Duck snuck in a spatula. Ruby cracked her egg on the slide. Flying Duck flipped it once. She flipped it again. Then she tried to scramble it. But the egg did not cook.

Each day they tried something new. It was a regular cooking show! The Recess Chefs, starring Ruby and Flying Duck. They had a taro cake. Then a pot sticker. Neither sizzled. The hot dog just sat there. And the frozen

Tater Tots didn't do much, either. But when Ruby brought in a hamburger, it began to ooze.

Cooking on the slide was so interesting that no one saw the playground monitor when he came over. So Ruby got busted. Again. And so did Flying Duck.

But getting busted in summer school was not as bad as getting busted in regular school. No one called anyone's parents. There was no emergency meeting in the principal's office.

Of course, the chefs had to clean their mess. They also had to make a sign:

NO COOKING OR FOOD ALLOWED ON THE PLAYGROUND.

It was posted, appropriately, near the hot, sizzling slide.

Even without Ruby and Flying Duck's cooking show, there was still a surprise of some kind every day.

One day a little snake showed up to play hopscotch.

Another day a rotten egg mysteriously appeared in the foursquare court.

Another day a mouse died on the doorstep.

Best of all, the daily surprise somehow always made it to class with Ruby or Flying

Duck for show-and-tell. And most days Miss Yamada, who had taught summer school before and was quite accustomed to surprises, would have something interesting to say about the offering.

"Sulfur is what makes the egg smell bad."

"Rigor mortis has set in," she said, gently tucking the dead mouse in a little box lined with cotton. "The poor thing has been dead for hours."

Miss Yamada was very smart. She made everyone feel important, even a dead mouse. Ruby loved her.

Ruby also loved Mentor Man. He taught Math with a Vengeance! Ruby loved Math with a Vengeance! She signed up for Addition with Attitude, Subtraction Without Sweat, and Multiplication Without Mumbling. Ruby could hardly stop doing math.

Flying Duck also loved summer school. There was a special class just for her: American Sign Language. But she wasn't the only one in the class. All the hearing children had signed up for it too, including Ruby.

Everyone wanted to learn a "secret language."

Flying Duck was very pleased.

"Hello!" Everyone

waved their open right hands several times.

"Friend." Both pointer fingers interlocked, separated, exchanged positions, and came together again as before.

"Thank you." The fingertips of one or both hands touched the lips, then moved forward until the palms were facing up, like they were blowing a kiss.

Ruby paid attention. She was getting better at sign. She was even bilingual! She remembered how to say "thank you" in Chinese sign, by wiggling her thumbs. Suddenly she discovered that she could wiggle her thumbs and blow kisses at the same time, while standing up, sitting down, or even while walking around!

"Wow!" she said. She showed the class.

"I'm fluent!" Ruby cried. "Do like me!"

And they did. It was the second-best pandemonium in summer school history.

But the truly best thing about summer school was this: Flying Duck got to meet other immigrant children. Trong was from

Vietnam. Mateo was from Columbia. Akiko was from Japan. And Youngja was from everywhere.

The immigrant students drew pictures of places they missed. And friends they had left behind. They longed for candy they couldn't find anymore. And taught one another games from other playgrounds. And sang silly songs from far away.

Together, they felt less homesick. Immigration became less scary. Even for Ruby.

10

A Dream Come True

Summer was finally coming to an end on 20th Avenue South.

The vapor of plums seeped into the house.

The breath of Chinese vegetables filled the garden.

Ruby's parents were not good at gardening, but Flying Duck's parents were expert farmers. They planted *gailan*, *yu choy*, *bok choy*, bitter melon, and *dong gua*. Ruby had never seen so many Chinese vegetables before. She and Flying Duck were expert farmers too. The girls especially liked Flying Duck's mother's "helpful exercises for relieving gardening stress," which included fanning oneself under the plum tree while sipping a glass of lemonade.

Flying Duck's parents hadn't found jobs yet, but they were getting closer. Everyone said that fall was a better time to look for work.

Ruby and Emma were friends again.

Emma and Flying Duck were friends at last.

So Ruby crossed off:

4. ~~Be frends again with Emma.~~*
5. ~~Play with Flying Duck.~~

And

7. ~~Go to summer skool.~~*

Wow. Ruby could hardly believe it. Now the only thing left was:

6. Play with Oscar.

That was easy.

"Come here, Oscar!" Ruby called. "OS-CAR!"

No sooner had Ruby called than a nose poked through the hole in the screen door. It sniffed.

"Oscar?"

"Rrrrf, rrrrrrf, rrrrfffff!" it barked.

It sounded like Oscar. It smelled like Oscar.

But it wasn't Oscar.

Ruby gasped. She clasped her chest. It was the cutest, sweetest little dog she had ever seen.

He had a mouthful of yellow teeth and

big clumsy feet and a big clumsy head and a big clumsy tail. His breath smelled like the end of the world, and his fur looked even worse.

Okay, so he wasn't the cutest. And he wasn't that little. In fact, he was quite big. Still, he was sweet. And he looked like an oversized mop.

He panted heavily.

Ruby forgot all about Oscar.

This was the dog Ruby had waited for all her life. She had looked for him every summer, but never found him. She had wished for him upon every star. She had breathed his name upon every wishbone. She had wanted him more than anything. He was a dream come true.

Instantly Ruby loved him. And so did Flying Duck. And so did Oscar.

There was only one little problem.

Emma.

Emma didn't love him. She loved Elwyn, who had been the only dog on 20th Avenue South for as long as anyone could remember. And Emma knew all there was to know about dogs.

"He's a stray," Emma said. "You can't play with a stray."

"He isn't a stray," Ruby replied. "He's mine. And his name is . . . is . . ."

"See, he doesn't even have a name!" Emma said. "And he has no tags," she added.

Tags were not a problem. There was enough aluminum foil in Ruby's kitchen to tag a million dogs. Flying Duck was good at cutting, and Ruby was good at writing.

But coming up with the right name was a little trickier.

Elmo? . . . Elmer? . . . Elonzo?

"Elvis!" Ruby called.

"Rrrrroooooh," crooned Elvis.

"What kind of a name is that?" Emma protested.

"Same kind as Elwyn," Ruby said.

"But Elwyn's a bona fide pet dog from the pet store," Emma said.

"Well, Elvis came from heaven," Ruby replied.

So Emma had something else to say.

"He has to have shots," Emma said, letting it sink in.

"Rabies, Lyme disease, distemper"—she rattled them off— "parvovirus, coronavirus, hepatitis, parainfluenza, Bordetella."

A dark, ripe plum fell close by. *Phump!*

Shots?

It was all Ruby could do not to jump Emma. Instead she counted to ten. Her father had taught her that when you're angry, count to ten.

When Ruby got to twenty, she still didn't feel any better. She felt like a latte machine bursting with hot, steamed milk.

Then the latte machine exploded.

"I should have never rescued you, Emma!" Ruby shrieked. "You. Belong. At the. Bottom. Of the. Pool!"

Emma let out a little cry.

Several dark, ripe plums fell. *Phump, phum-phum, phump!*

And then it was quiet.

Very quiet.

"Wait till your mother finds out what you said," Emma said, blinking back tears. "Not to mention when she sees the stray. You're going to be *so* busted."

Then Emma gathered Sam and Elwyn, and she did exactly as Ruby was hoping

she'd do. She
went home.

Ruby
thought she
would feel
better. She'd
given Emma
what Emma
deserved.

But Ruby didn't feel so good.

She didn't feel like a latte machine
anymore.

She didn't even feel like a regular
coffeemaker.

Ruby felt terrible.

Why did Emma always have to ruin
everything? Everything had been perfect.
Their friendship was on again and they
were cruising along. But now it was off

again, and it was like having a dead battery in your car.

It seemed their friendship had gone to the dogs. Ruby loved that expression. Gone to the dogs.

But worst of all, Emma was on to something. Ruby's mother was not home. What would she say when she saw Elvis? A three-hundred-pound Elvis?

Ruby had to think fast.

11

Empress of Everything

Aluminum foil has many uses.

It is clothing for a potato.

It is a hand warmer. Wrap your hands in aluminum foil. Sit in sun.

It is a foot warmer. Do the same as above, except on your feet.

It is a hair warmer. Do the same as above, except on your hair. Sit in beauty parlor. Read magazines. Ruby had seen her mother do this, and her hair always came out like sunshine.

It is a TV antenna-extender. Ruby's GungGung had done this.

It is a pet tag.

It is the source of all sorts of crown jewels. Fold this way for a crown. Scrunch this way into a scepter. Smooth it out for a sword.

"I crown thee Prince Oscar the Cutie," Ruby declared, placing an aluminum crown on Oscar's head and giving him the appropriate taps on the shoulder with her foil sword.

Turning to her cousin, "I crown thee Princess First Duck Flying in a V," Ruby said. Flying Duck bowed, which made her crown fall off.

Then Ruby thought about Emma. For a fleeting moment Ruby thought about how much Emma would enjoy getting crowned and wearing lots of magical jewelry. But then the thought was gone.

"And I crown myself . . . ," Ruby said. She had to think about this one a little more. It had to be something appropriate. It couldn't be anything fake or too important. But, of course, it had to be wonderful.

"Okay, I got it!" Ruby cried. "I crown myself . . . Empress . . . of Everything!" It was perfect. And her crown fit just right.

Now, as everyone knows, empresses are very powerful.

Their jewelry has magical powers.

It took a little practice, but soon Ruby and Flying Duck were working all sorts of magic with their royal scepters.

Take Ruby's mother, for example. She

was reading on the couch. Ruby aimed her scepter directly at her.

With the dog hidden in the garage out back, the empress had time to work her magic.

"My royal mother looks sleepy," the empress intoned, waving her scepter from across the room.

"My royal mother should nap instead of read. . . ." The empress shot powerful rays out of her eyes.

Meanwhile, Flying Duck and Oscar marched around and around the royal sofa.

"Sweeeep," Oscar bubbled. "Sweeeep." He meant "sleep." He looked his mother smack in the eye and then wiggled his thumbs at her. He was so cute.

It took forever. But finally her royal mother was napping. And so were Princess Flying Duck and Prince Oscar, who curled up with his royal mother and fell fast asleep. Ruby nearly fell under her own spell too, it was that powerful. But she had a job to finish. After all, you can't be Empress of Everything and snooze, too!

"You *love* dogs," Ruby began, standing over her sleeping mother.

"You love BIG dogs," she intoned.

"You will see Elvis," Ruby added for good measure, "and fall in love!"

Then she paused. She looked closely at her mother's sleeping face. Ruby had rarely seen her mother asleep. She looked beautiful with her eyes closed. She did not snore.

"I love you, Mom," Ruby whispered. She gave her a kiss.

Then it was back to work. Being Empress of Everything was a big job. Ruby repeated everything she said before about dogs. Mind control is like that. For best results, you have to repeat several times, like medicine.

Ruby tiptoed out to the garage to check on Elvis. Then she tiptoed back to watch her kingdom sleep.

She watched.

And watched.

And watched. . . .

"Aaaaaaaaaaaaaack!"

Ruby woke with a start. Oh no! She had fallen asleep too!

And Elvis, who had apparently tiptoed back in with Ruby, was licking Ruby's mother's face!

And Ruby's mother screamed! *"Aaaaack! Aaaaack!"*

Oscar woke and started crying.

Flying Duck jumped and starting signing.

"Oh no!" Ruby cried. She and Flying Duck grabbed their dog and pulled him back. But it was too late.

"Ruby! What . . . what . . . what is that?" Ruby's mother stammered.

"A dog," Ruby said.

"A BIG dog," Ruby added quickly, to open the floodgates of love. She crossed her fingers to boost her mother's learn-while-you-sleep abilities.

Ruby's mother clutched Oscar.

"Call the police!

"Call the animal shelter!

"Where's the vacuum cleaner?

Then finally . . .

"That's no dog!" her mother shrieked. "That's Dogzilla!"

12

20/20 Vision

Everything happens the week before school starts.

Posters of DOG FOUND: ANSWERS TO ELVIS AND DOGZILLA went up all over 20th Avenue South.

Ruby's father placed an ad in the newspaper.

Meanwhile Elvis got shampooed.

He got clipped.

He got brushed.

He even got shots.

But he didn't get real tags . . . yet.

Still, Ruby was hopeful. Every day that passed without someone coming forward to claim Elvis was another day closer to Elvis staying forever. Ruby had heard about this happening to other dogs, and she was sure that it would happen to him. She kept her fingers crossed.

Meanwhile summer school ended.

Swimming school closed.

Empty sunscreen bottles rattled around different corners of the house.

Then it rained for nights.

And it fogged for days. Everything was *moong-cha-cha*. Ruby loved that word, "*moong-cha-cha*." Her mother used it often. It meant not clear, out of focus, confused.

Everything was changing, even the weather.

Even Elvis. He got to come into the house. The garage was getting cold at night, Ruby's mother said. It had no doors.

Ruby's mother wasn't crazy about dogs, but Elvis had many human characteristics.

He needed his own blanket.

And his own bed.

And his own rice bowl.

And most of all, he needed to be near other people.

And when Elvis had all those things, it no longer mattered that no one had come forward to claim him. He was already claimed.

So Elvis became Elvis Lu, the newest member of Ruby's family and not a stray. It was one of the best changes of the season.

But one thing didn't change.

Ruby still hadn't made up with Emma.

Ruby didn't like to apologize. So she didn't.

But the wee little voice inside Ruby's head spoke to her about this nearly every day.

"Rubeeee . . ."

Uh-oh. Suddenly it was louder than Ruby remembered it.

"Rubeeeeeee!"

Ruby jumped. Her wee little voice was not usually so sharp and clear.

"Yes?" she peeped.

"I just found your *backpack*!"

It was not Ruby's wee little voice at all. It was Ruby's mother. She was standing on the back step with Ruby's backpack, the one long-forgotten in the back of her closet, the one from second grade, the one that held—gasp—the hidden letters! And her mother was waving them!

Oh no!

"Ruby, why didn't you give me these letters?" her mother cried.

"I didn't want to flunk," Ruby squeaked.

"What? These are from the nurse's office," Ruby's mother screeched. "You and Flying Duck need to have your eyes checked. You both need glasses, *aiyaaaah!*"

Eyes checked?

Glasses?

"Hooray!" Ruby cried. She would finally get glasses!

So that afternoon Ruby and Flying Duck got glasses. Ruby chose a cute little pair with . . . what else? . . . sparkly rubies! And Flying Duck picked the frame with the twinkly diamonds.

Suddenly nothing was *moong-cha-cha* anymore. Everything was clear! Ruby felt like a new person with glasses. She was not the person she was before. Teachers wear glasses. Mah-jongg masters wear glasses. Scientists wear glasses.

Benjamin Franklin wore glasses.

Now Ruby wore glasses. And so did Flying Duck.

Wow.

Ruby puffed out her chest like a pigeon.

She was ready for third grade.

Almost.

13

The Emma Dilemma

The whole world is different when you have 20/20 vision.

Ruby found she loved to listen to marching band music. It was GungGung's favorite music, and Oscar's too. Now Ruby loved it. It made her feel confident. She could march and see where she was going, all at the same time.

Everything was much clearer to Ruby. Even friendships.

Yes, she was ready to march right over to Emma's house and be friends again.

Oh, no, she wasn't. She was simply ready to march to her plum tree and sit in it.

Alone.

Suddenly her plum tree felt like the biggest plum tree in the world.

And Ruby was the teeniest, tiniest little bird.

It was a good place to think things over.

Would her tree always feel this empty if she never, *ever* apologized?

A gentle breeze combed Ruby's feathers.

Why was friendship so hard?

Ruby blinked a little bird blink.

She moved her foot, just a little, like a bird getting a better hold.

Leaves broke into applause.

Why did summer have to end?

Ruby didn't know.

But she knew what she had to do.

She put on a little John Philip Sousa to

get warmed up. And she let her legs march
her right next door.

"Em-ma!!" Ruby called from
Emma's front stoop. She
marched in place. It was
more fun than marching forward. Ruby could lift her
knees as high as her arm-
pits.

Emma appeared imme-
diately from behind her
door.

"Emma . . . ," Ruby
said, breathless.
She wanted
Emma to see
her marching
t e c h n i q u e .
Then she stopped. She
swallowed. She stood on one foot . . .

then she stood on another. She wiggled a little, but not too much.

"I am truly glad I saved your life," she finally said.

Then Ruby stopped to think. She had more to say. In fact she could feel an entire speech coming.

"You deserve to be saved over and over again," Ruby declared. "I hope we can be friends again."

Emma thought about it. "Okay," she said.

Ruby paused. She searched for something else to say. Something friendly. Maybe even something impressive. But she couldn't think of a single thing.

But Emma came up with something.

"I think I can march like that too," Emma said.

"Really?"

"Sure!" Emma showed Ruby. She was pretty good. She'd never even marched before.

Ruby joined her. Together they marched in place. Emma could lift her knees up to her armpits too. And several times she even got them up to the bottoms of her earlobes. It was utterly breathtaking.

"Nice height," Ruby huffed. She could hardly get her words out, but she meant it.

"Nice glasses," Emma puffed.

Ruby grinned. And Emma grinned back.

After that Ruby put a smiley face next to:

4. ~~Be frends again with Emma.~~* ☺

It was the perfect ending to a perfect summer.

Now Ruby could hardly wait for third grade.

Her backpack was cleaned out.

Her glasses were on.
She was finally ready.

That night, as Ruby and Flying Duck waited in their bunk beds for sleep to overtake them, the stars in their window moved from their summer positions to their fall ones. With her glasses on, Ruby could see this very clearly. She and Flying Duck wore their glasses to sleep so that they could see their dreams.

But what was that across the room? Right there under her window was . . . a stack of books!

Oh no! It was the very thing Ruby couldn't put her knuckle on when she had made her summer list! At last, the very important thing that should have been on her 12-Step Plan:

Her summer reading.

RUBY'S and FLYING DUCK'S
Amazing and Awesome Glossaries

Ruby's Amazing Glossary and Guide to Important Words

aquaphobia—A life-threatening fear of drowning during swimming lessons while wearing all your PFDs (*see* PFD).

aquaphobic—Someone who suffers from the above.

Basic Lifesaving—Watch at your own risk.

bok choy—A leafy green and white vegetable. Leaves can be used for fanning oneself.

Bordetella—A bad germ that causes dogs to cough.

busted—A fate worse than death.

Cantonese—Language needed to order yummy Chinese food. But also shouted by parents when you are busted. Also used in Chinese school.

Coral Cay—Where the better-than-beginner swimmers go.

coronavirus—Doggie vomit and diarrhea.

cross-chest carry—Used to save a drowning person. Throw your arm across their chest and under the opposite armpit, hug them close, and swim to safety.

distemper—Not the same as "bad temper" or "losing your temper." Worse than it sounds. Affects dogs. Includes fever; loss of appetite; thick, yellow slime from eyes and nose; coughing; and seizures.

dong gua—Big watermelon–type melon that grows a chalky white dust on its skin.

e-mail—Do-it-yourself, easy mail. No stamps. No mail delivery person. Just type and click! Grandparents love it.

Elvis—Dog wonder.

Emma—Best friend wonder.

Flying Duck—Cousin wonder.

gailan—A leafy green-only vegetable. Too limp for fanning.

goose bumps—A radar system for detecting

anything scary or dangerous or wonderful or breathtakingly beautiful.

GungGung (sounds like "goong goong")—Grandpa on your mother's side.

hepatitis—A bad fever in your liver (*see* liver).

Iorana koe—"Hello" or "good-bye" in Rapa Nui to just one buddy.

Iorana korua—"Hello" or "good-bye" to more than one buddy.

latte—Rhymes with "karate." Tastes like karate too. Coffee topped with frothy steamed milk. Do not feed to babies.

liver—One of your guts. Looks like the bottom of a shoe.

Lyme disease—Makes you feel five hundred years old. Caused by a deer tick bite.

mah-jongg—A very noisy game of matching tiles that usually involves yummy snacks and ends with Second Uncle hanging spoons from his face.

midjump—The worst place to be caught.

moong-cha-cha—Not clear. Fuzzy in the head or in the eyes. Not focused.

Motorboat Lane—Where advanced swimmers speed by like motorboats.

Oscar—Cutest baby brother in the world. Mostly.

parainfluenza—Coughing, sneezing, wheezing. Highly contagious among dogs.

parvovirus—Doggy diarrhea.

PFD—Personal flotation device. Includes life jackets, water wings, waist buoys, float belts, anything that keeps you from drowning while holding on to the side of the pool. Very useful.

Poh-Poh (sounds like "paw paw")—Grandma on your mother's side.

rabies—A bad germ that will kill you but makes you go crazy first.

Rapa Nui—Where the superduper advanced swimmers go. A cute little island in the Pacific Ocean. Looks like the world's belly button. Also the language spoken there.

Ruby—A precious gem. Empress of Everything.

Shallow Shores—Where aquaphobics go to try to get over their aquaphobia.

Smile Buddy—The best job in the whole world next to being empress.

John Philip Sousa—The best composer in the world next to Wolfgang Amadeus Mozart.

UtterPrincess—The best doll in the world next to nothing.

yu choy—A leafy green vegetable. Not fanning material either.

Flying Duck's Awesome Glossary and Guide to Important Chinese Sign Language Signs

(as demonstrated by Ruby)

"I burst my skull"—
Tap head and make a
burst of fireworks with
outspread fingers behind ears.

"More"—Put first finger and thumb
together and move hand to opposite side
of chest. Then pull hand across chest
sideways, ending in a number one sign.

"Eat"—Put first finger and middle finger together, and touch fingertips to lips multiple times with fingers pointing sideways.

"Sleep"—Make a fist, rest head on fingers.

"Dog"—Make a "mouth" using the thumb and fingers of one hand and "ears" using the first finger and middle finger of the other, and place the "ears" on top of the "mouth."

"Help"—Raise hands at sides with palms facing outward, then rotate arms down to waist, so palms are facing the floor.

"I'm sorry"—
Salute person with left hand, then touch left pinky to chest over and over.

"Hello"—Wave open right hand several times.

"Thank you"—Wiggle thumbs at knuckles.

And Flying Duck's favorite American Sign Language sign:

"Friend"—Interlock pointer fingers, separate, then exchange their positions, and come together again as before.